ASPEN'S
MAGICAL MERMAID
NECKLACE

Cole,
Find the magic in
everything you do! x
Mel Ahonen

Written by
Melissa Ahonen

Illustrated by
Daria Shamolina

ASPEN'S MAGICAL MERMAID NECKLACE

Published by Dandelion Dreams Publishing (Melissa Ahonen, LLC)
www.melissaahonen.com
Lincoln, ND

Text and Illustration Copyright 2022: Melissa Ahonen. All rights reserved.
Edited by: Myriah C. Boudreaux

Library of Congress Control Number: 2022903055

ISBN: 978-1-7377121-4-5 (hardcover)
978-1-7377121-3-8 (paperback)

All inquiries of this book can be sent to the
author at melissa@melissaahonen.com.
For more information or to book an event,
please visit www.melissaahonen.com

Dandelion Dreams
PUBLISHING

This book is printed in the United States of America.

Aspen, my sassy and sweet girl.
Your imagination and creativity are contagious.
Dream big, Baby Girl, and you will move mountains.

Madge: You are the author of your own story.
Make sure you write a memorable one.
I am so glad I get to be part of your story.

"I cannot wait to play at the **beach**. Mom, when can we go?" Aspen bounces through the airport, eager to reach the sand and saltwater.

"I could see the whitecaps from the air!" Easton chimes in. "When can we surf?"

"Soon," Mom chuckles. "Very soon."

"We have to make it out of the airport first, you two," Dad says.

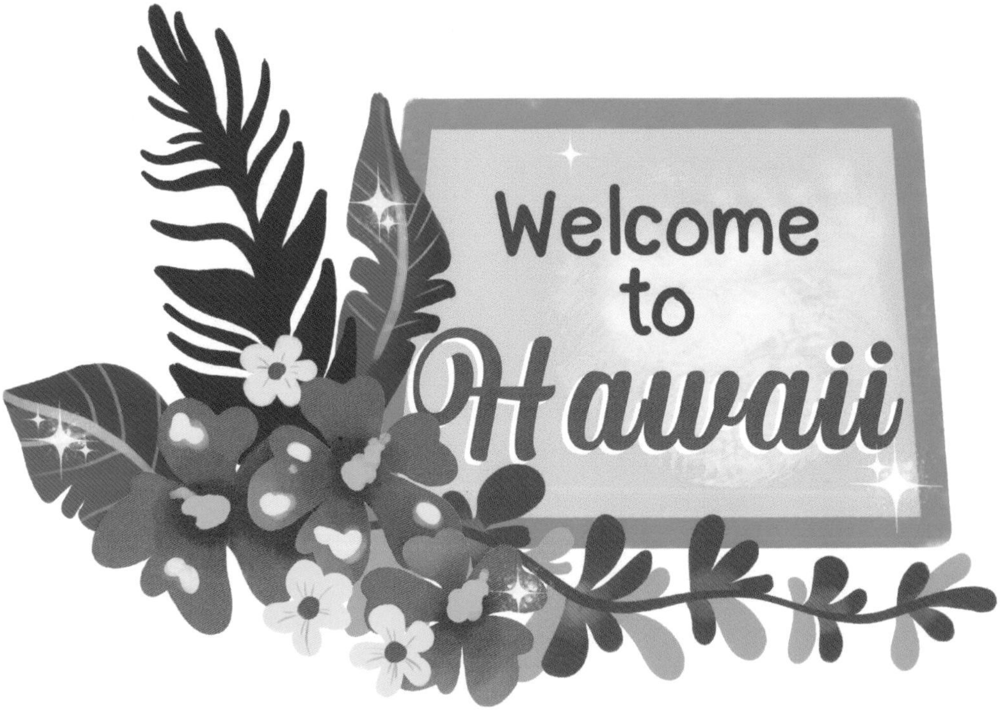
Welcome
to
Hawaii

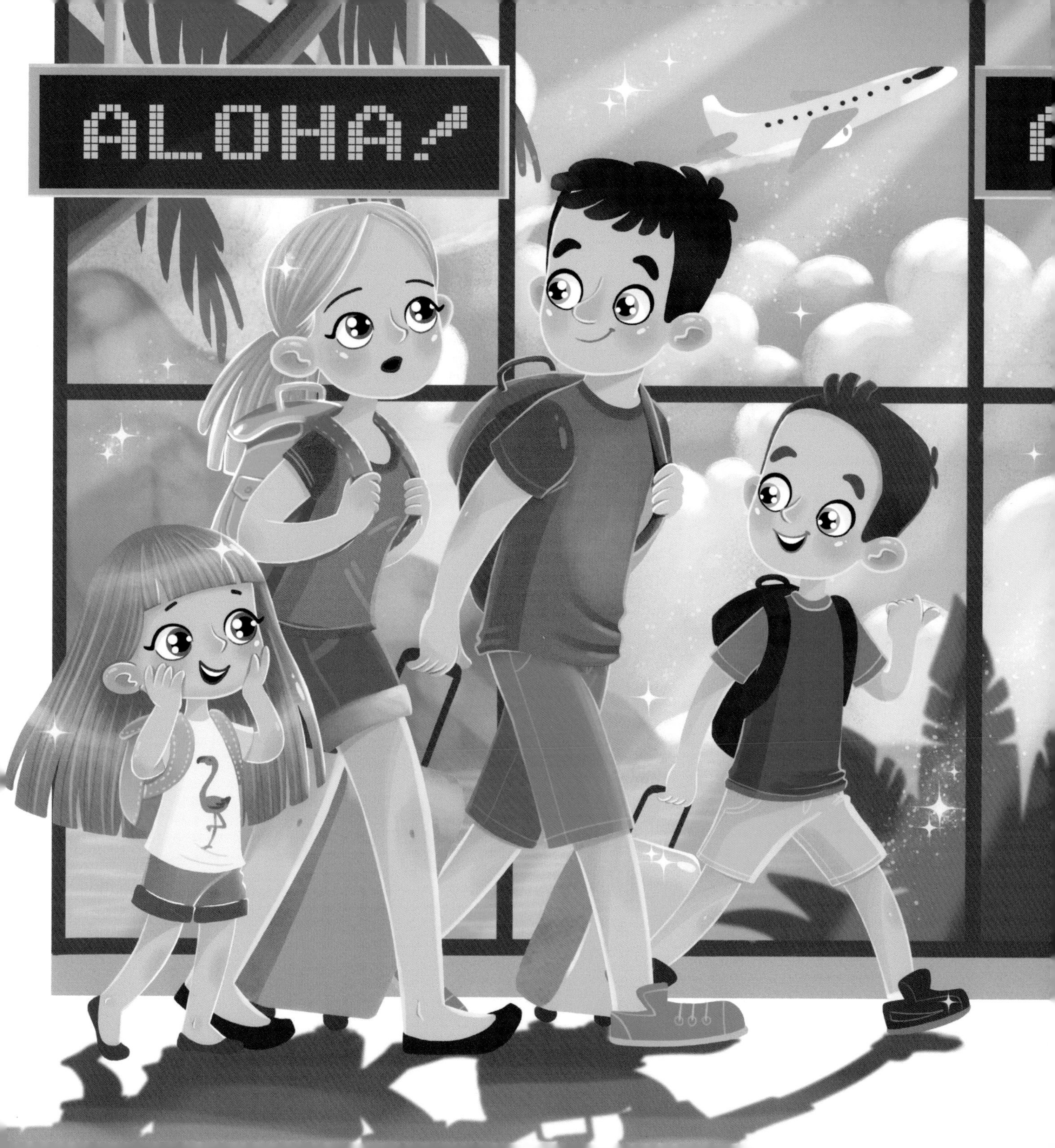
ALOHA!

Later that day, Aspen finds many unique shells and sets them in her bucket. She notices a large shell between two rocks and scoops it up. She realizes it's more than a shell. It's a NECKLACE.

Awestruck, Aspen whispers, "This is the most beautiful necklace I have ever seen." She clasps the necklace around her neck to keep it safe, then runs back to her family.

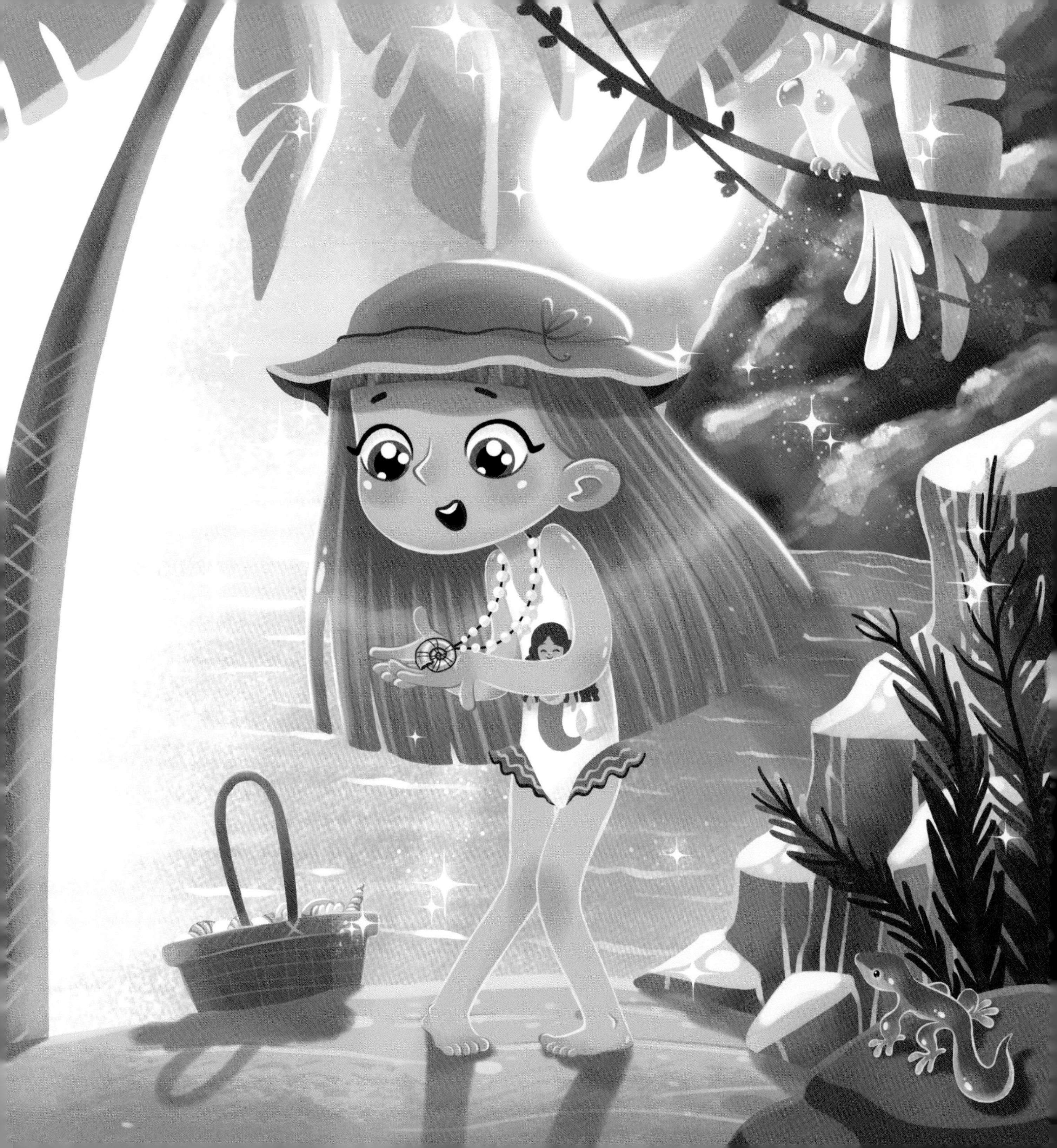

"Mom, **Dad!** Look what I **found!** It's looks like mermaid jewelry!" Aspen shows them the necklace. "I plan to keep it always!"

"That is very pretty," agrees Dad. "But what if someone is missing it?"

"I saved it from floating away!" Aspen protests. After a moment, she offers, "If no one has lost it, can I keep it? Please?"

"If no one claims it after we report it, it can be yours," Dad replies.

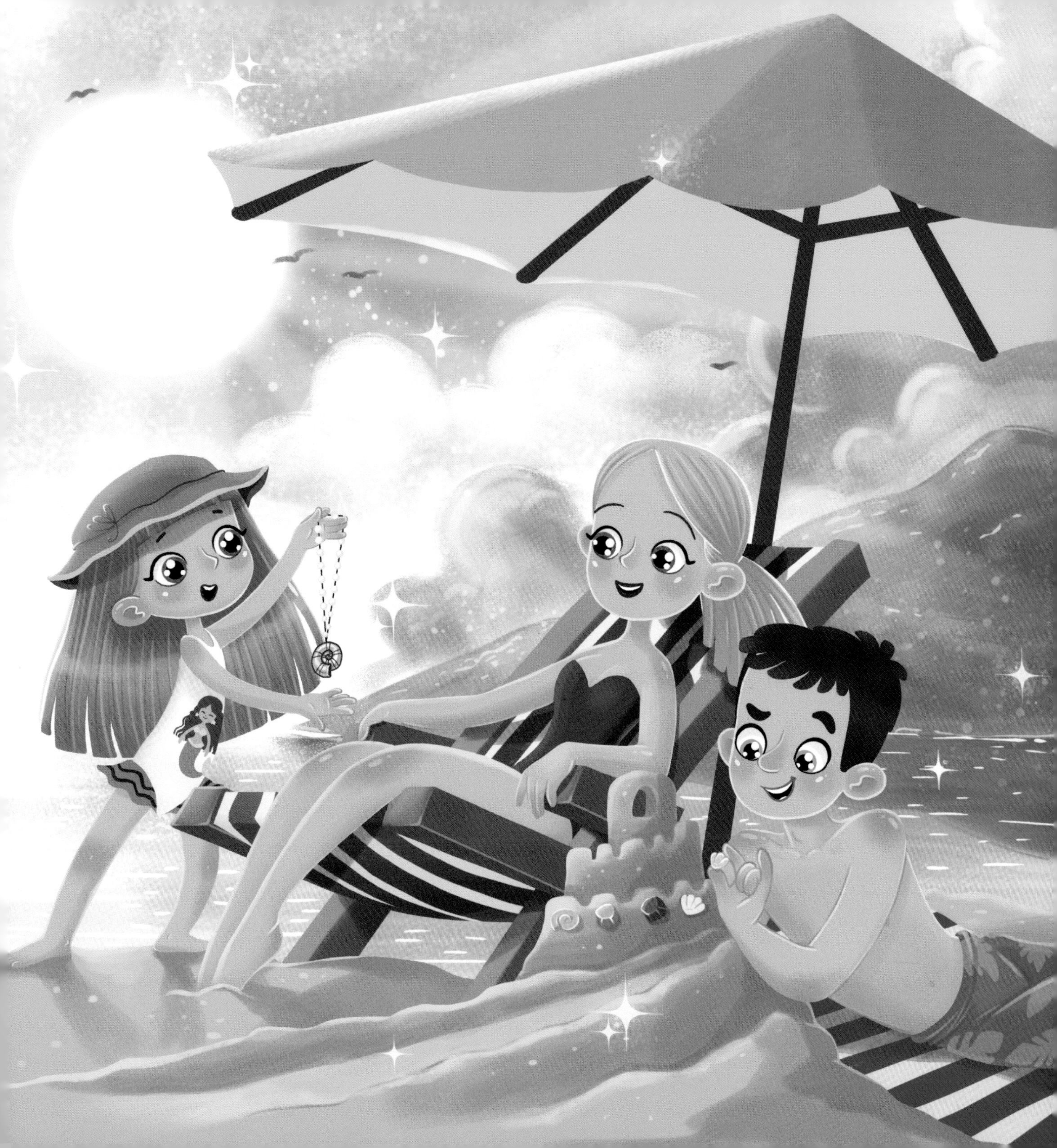

The next morning, Aspen and Easton are learning to surf, but Aspen keeps glancing around, unable to focus. She can't shake the feeling there's someone watching her.

"Aspen, come on. Try to ride a wave with me!" Easton calls.

Aspen paddles over, and the two of them catch an arching wave.

"**woohoo!** This is awesome, Easton!" Aspen cheers. Aspen starts doing tricks in the wave, astonishing everyone, including herself, about her new talent.

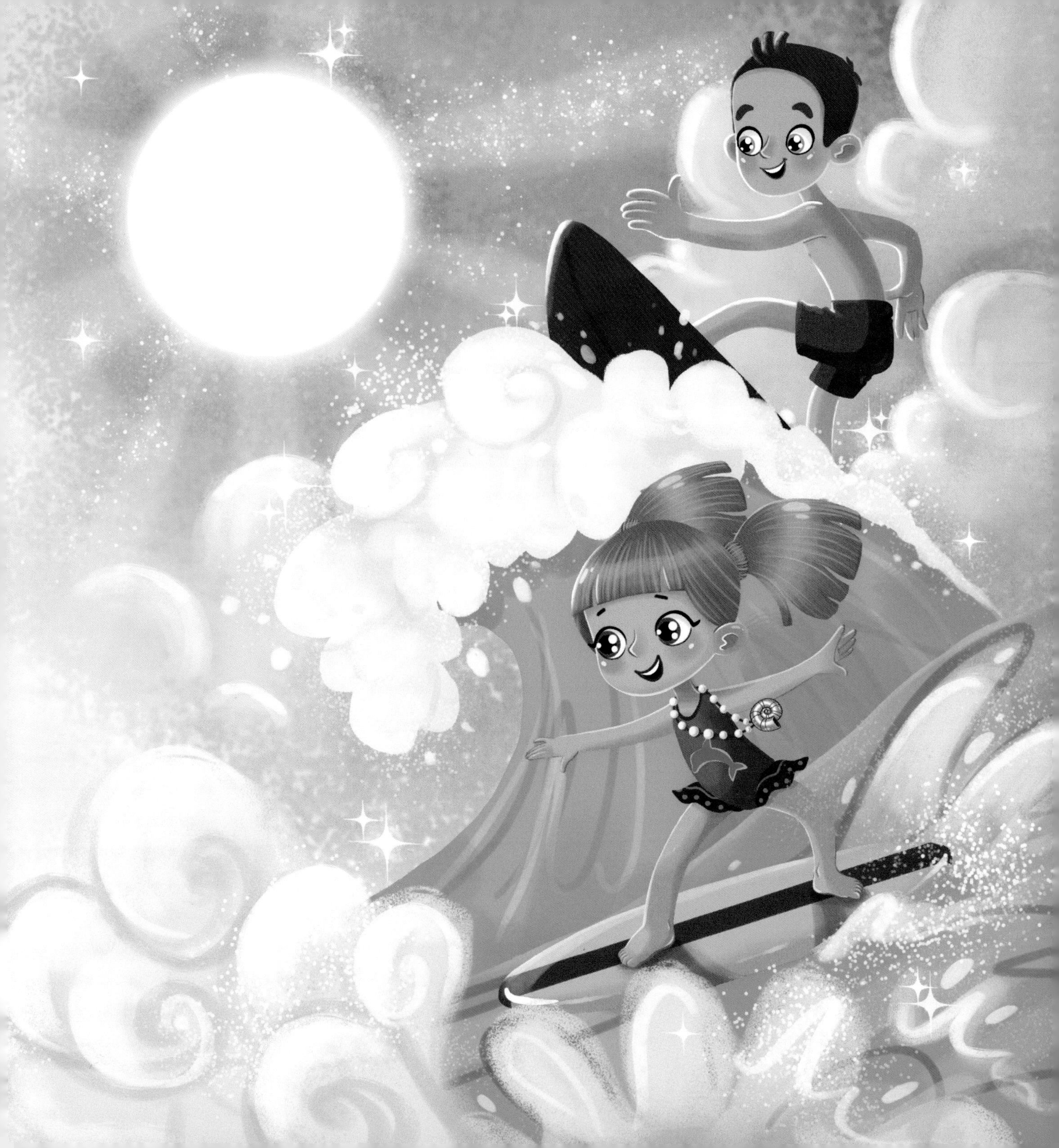

While snorkeling on the third day of their trip, Aspen spots a sparkly flipper in the water. As she swims closer, the water shines brighter. The light is coming from her necklace. It's **glowing!** She kicks to the surface to check the pendant. But it suddenly grows dark.

"Did you discover a scary fish?" Easton says, laughing. "You jumped right out of the water!"

"Easton, I think I saw a mermaid!" exclaims Aspen.

"Sure, you did." Easton tugs Aspen toward the boat. "The captain is calling everyone aboard. Come on. I'll race you back."

Aspen starts swimming. Her feet are paddling like little motors. To her surprise, she beats her big brother to the boat!

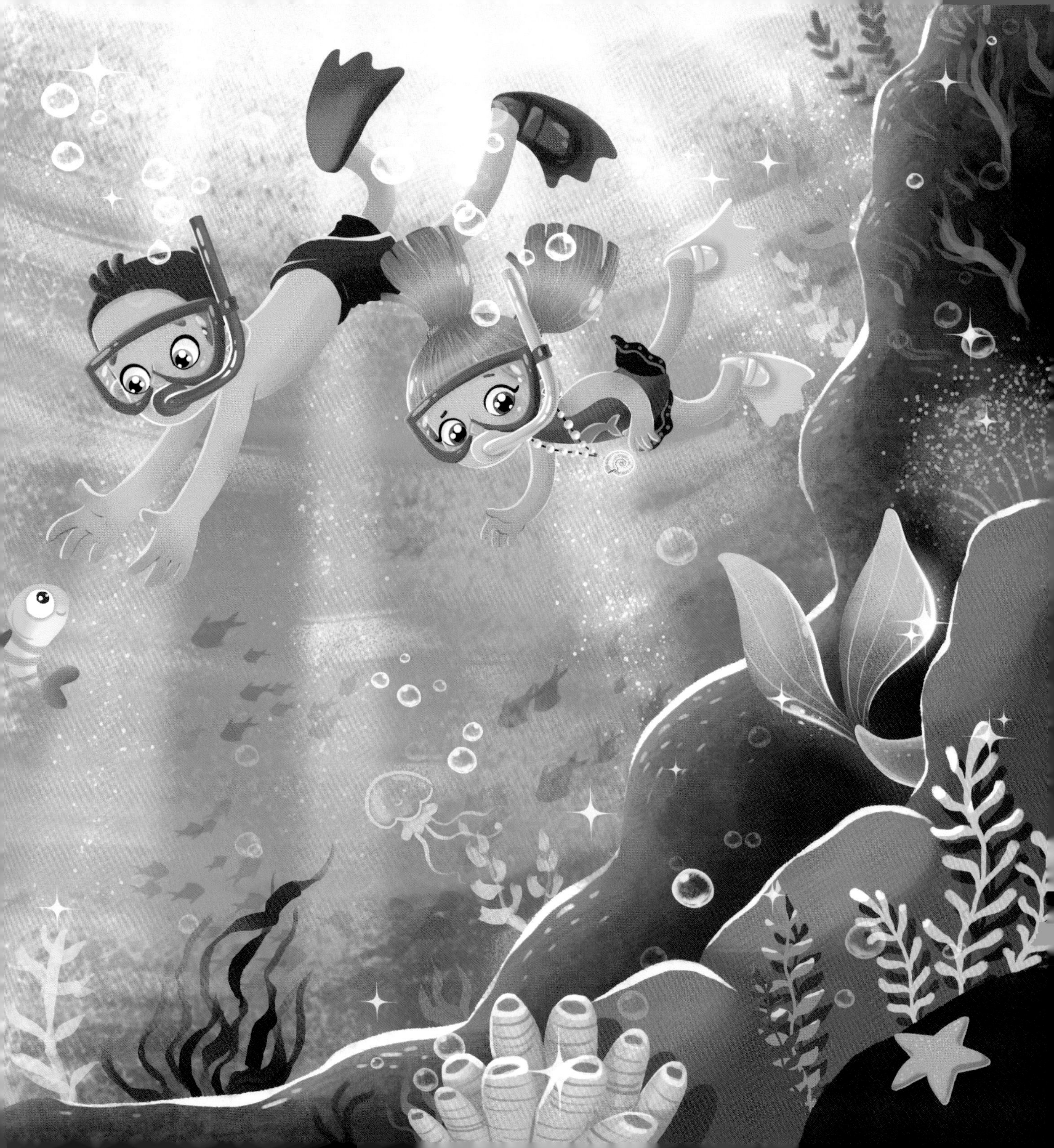

"Look at the dolphins!" Mom squeals, grabbing her camera. Dolphins are fun, but Aspen dreams of glimpsing a real mermaid. Her chances are running out with her family leaving tomorrow.

Just then, Aspen hears a squeaky *hello* as a dolphin jumps in the air right in front of her. Aspen squints and looks around, but no one is looking at her. Could she really be hearing dolphins speak?

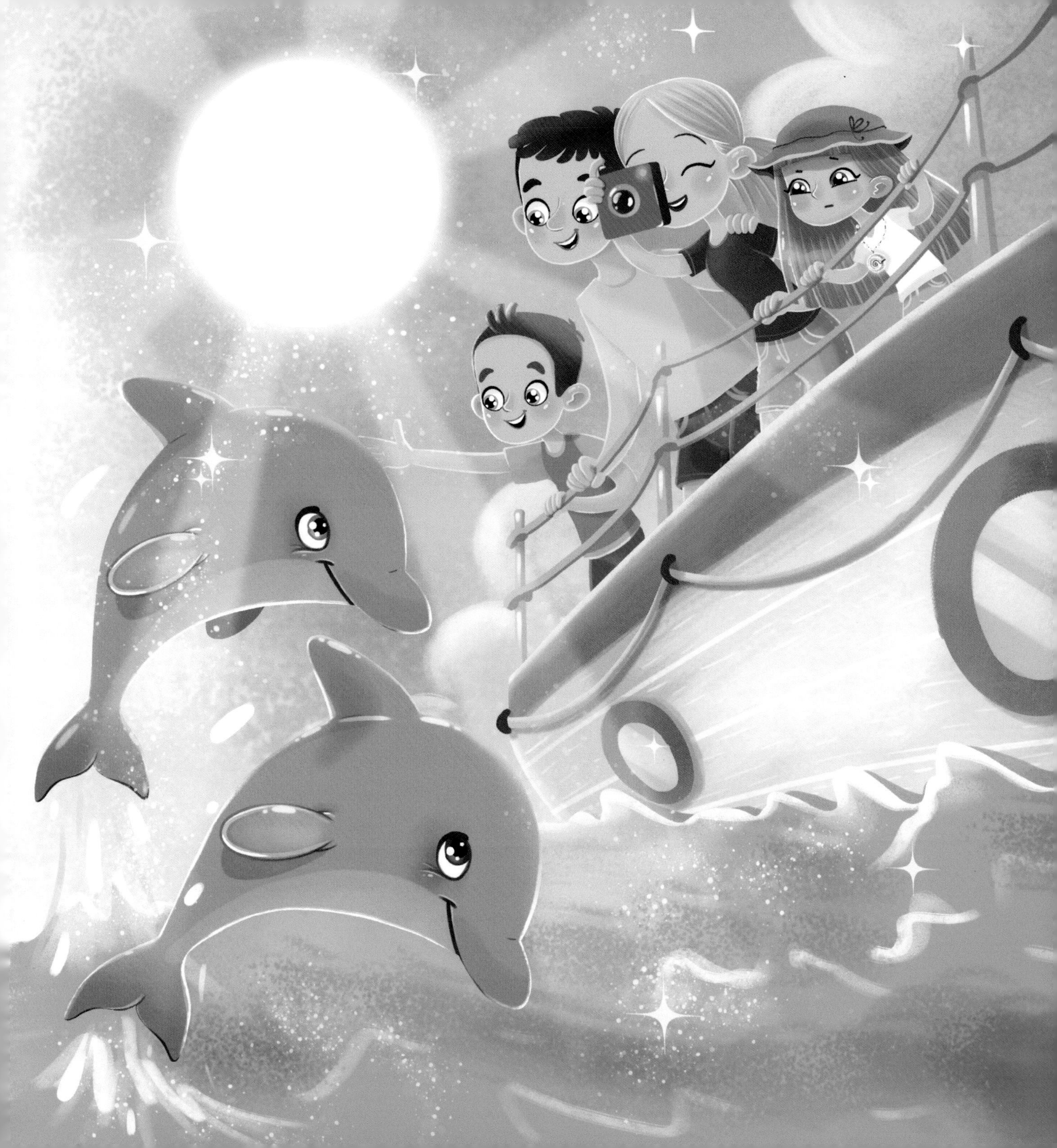

Mesmerized, Aspen moves along the boat to see the dolphin greeting her. "Hello dolphin! Are you speaking to me?"

"It's me! It's me, leaping out of the sea.
Hello! Hello!" the dolphin replies.

Aspen laughs in delight and is about to respond when she notices her necklace glowing again.

"It does glow! It's magical!"

Aspen clutches her necklace as it grows dark.
"Did you glow because someone is missing you?" she whispers.
"Hopefully, it was just a coincidence. I want to keep you forever!"

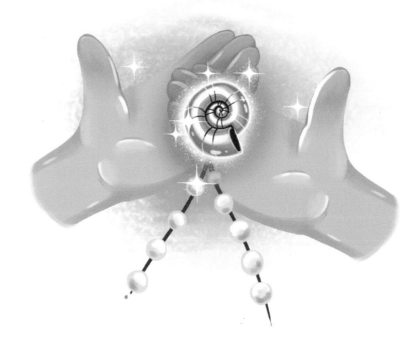

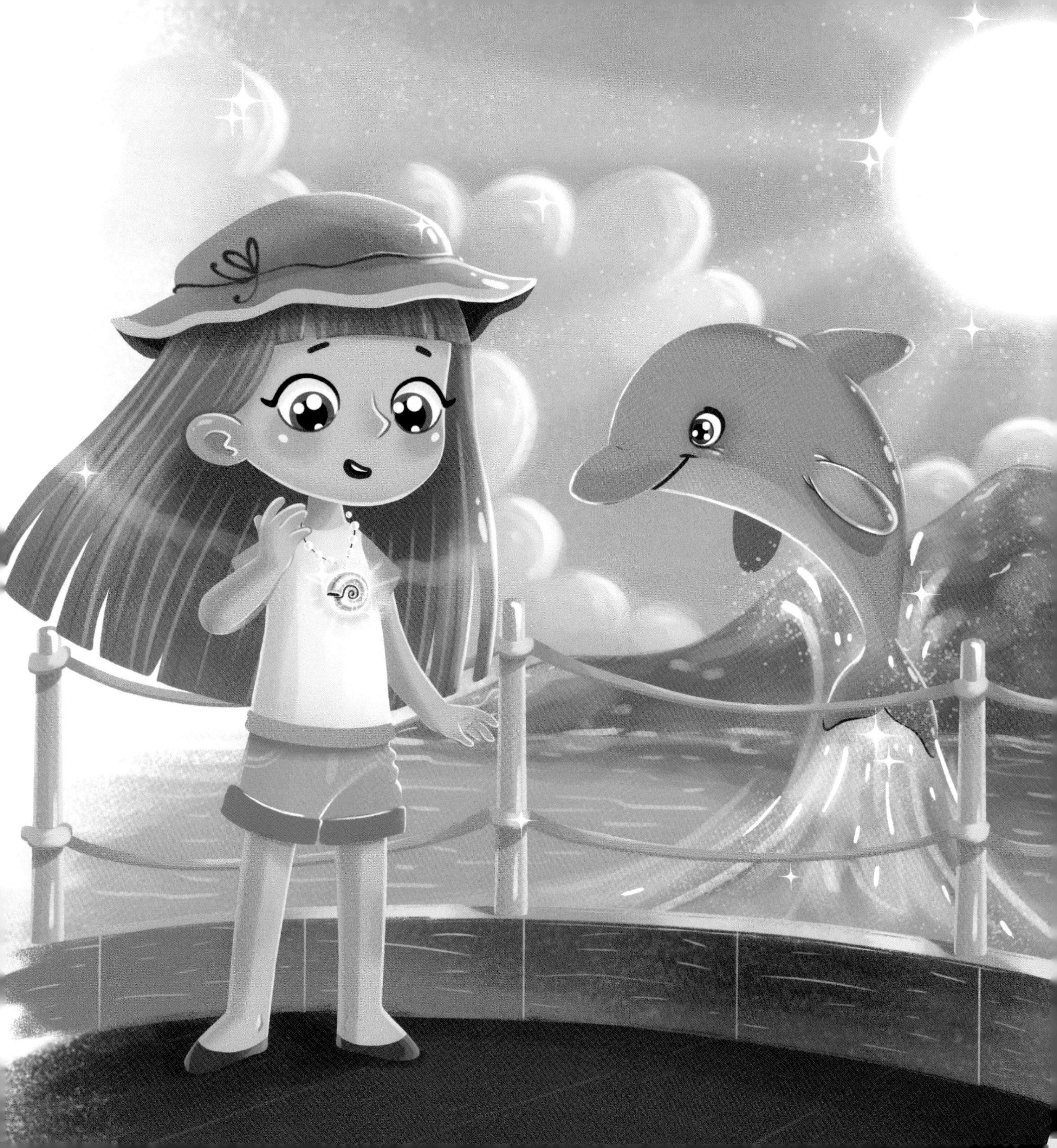

On the last day of the trip, Aspen shuffles along the tropical shore. She must say goodbye. But first, she makes a final visit to the spot where she rescued her necklace. She notices movement beside her and startles. A dazzling Mermaid sits atop the large rock!

Aspen gasps. "You're a real **mermaid!**"

"I am." The mermaid nods. "You're a real friend. Thank you for keeping my necklace safe. I'm Luna."

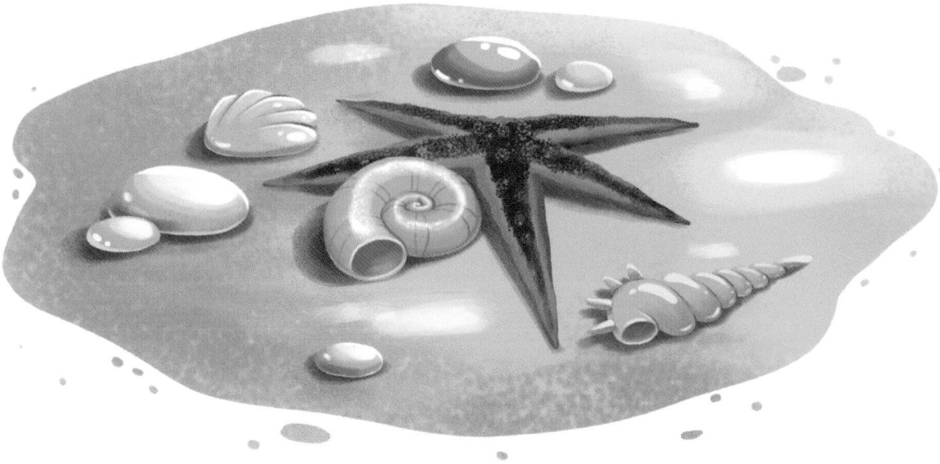

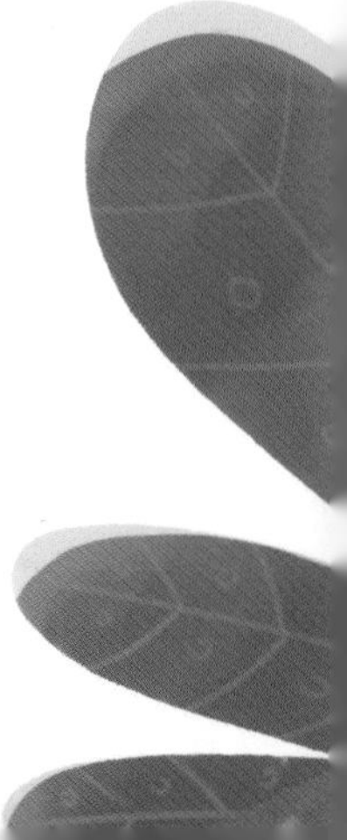

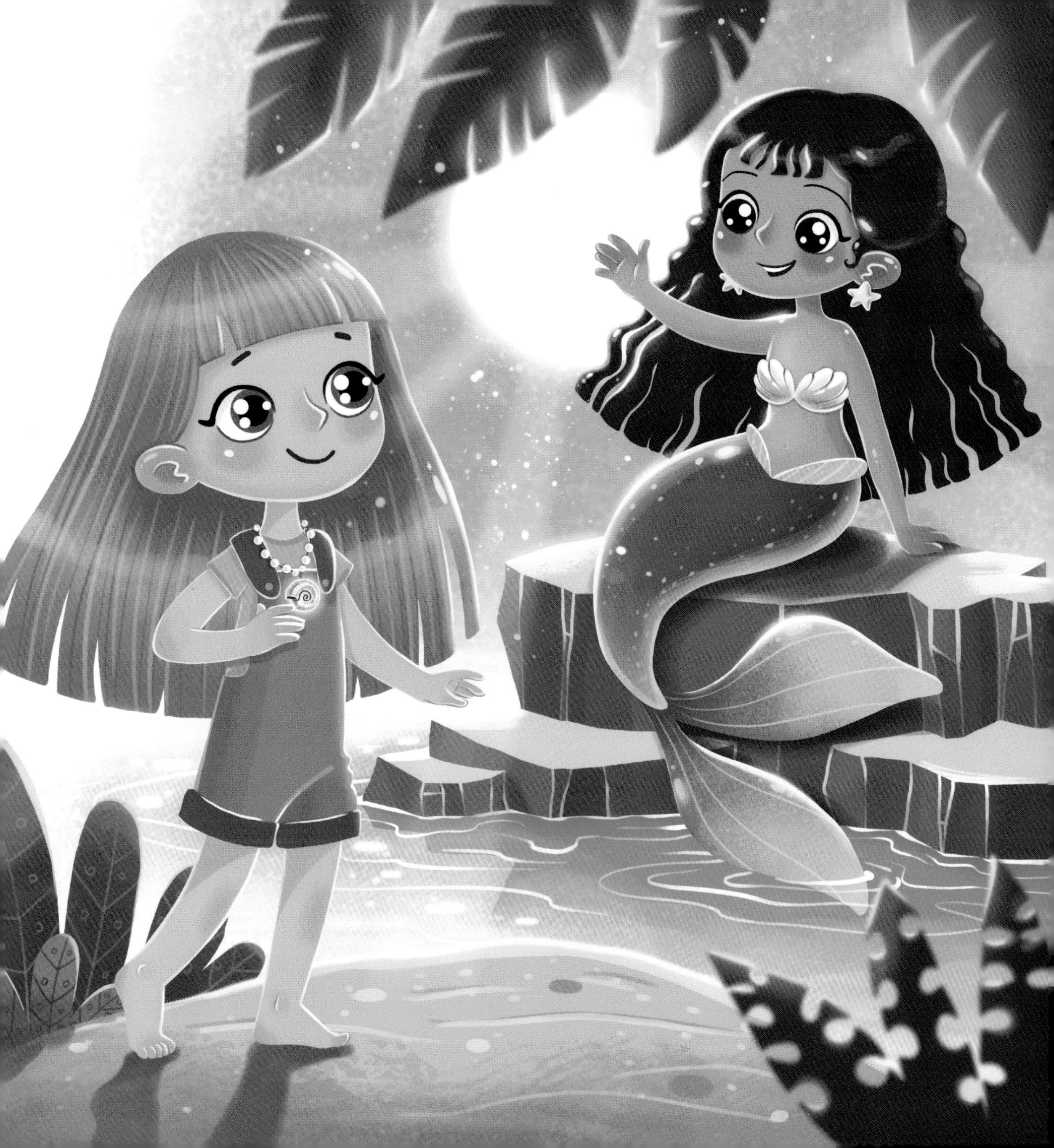

"I'm Aspen." Aspen approaches the mermaid as her necklace beams forth a dazzling light. She tilts her head, pondering. "Have you been watching me all week?"

"Yes, I wanted to thank you for keeping my necklace safe."

"Yes, I kept it," Aspen admits, gazing at the necklace. "It seems to glow sometimes."

"It glows when I am near," Luna explains. "The shell has magical powers for mermaids. It protects me."

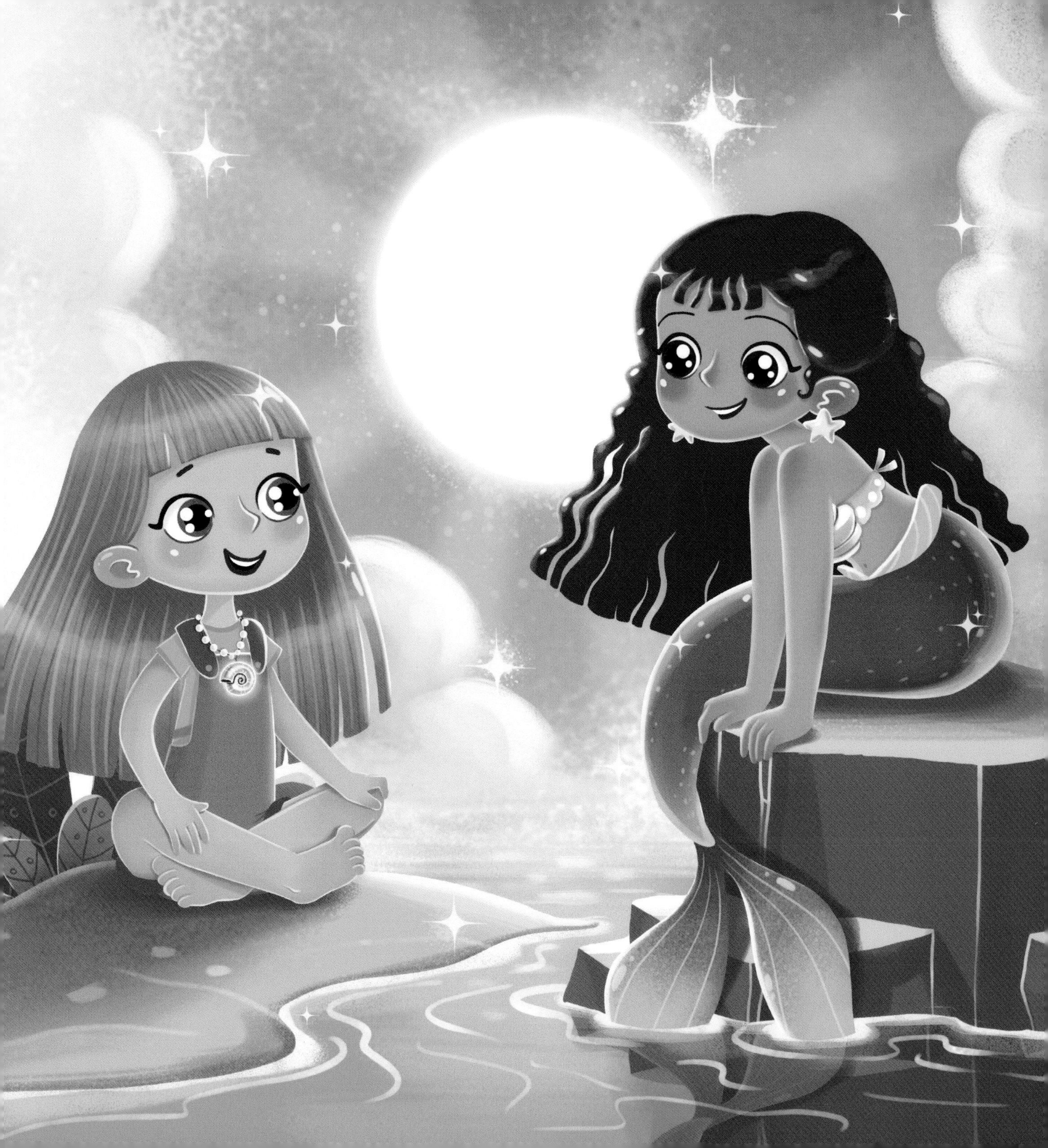

"I was right. It is **magical!** I have noticed some strange things lately. Was it the necklace that helped me surf right away and swim super-fast and hear the dolphins speak?" Aspen unclasps the necklace and looks from the bright shell to her mermaid friend.

"Yes, the necklace enables us to balance and swim well. It also allows us to hear dolphins since they are our special friends," says Luna, smiling.

Aspen clutches the necklace giving it a final squeeze. "I'm glad I could keep it safe for you." She reaches out to Luna. "But you need this to stay safe."

"Let's trade," says Luna. "Aspen, wear this next time you are here, and I will find you. It will glow whenever I am near."

"Amazing!" exclaims Aspen. "My very own mermaid necklace? Oh, thank you!"

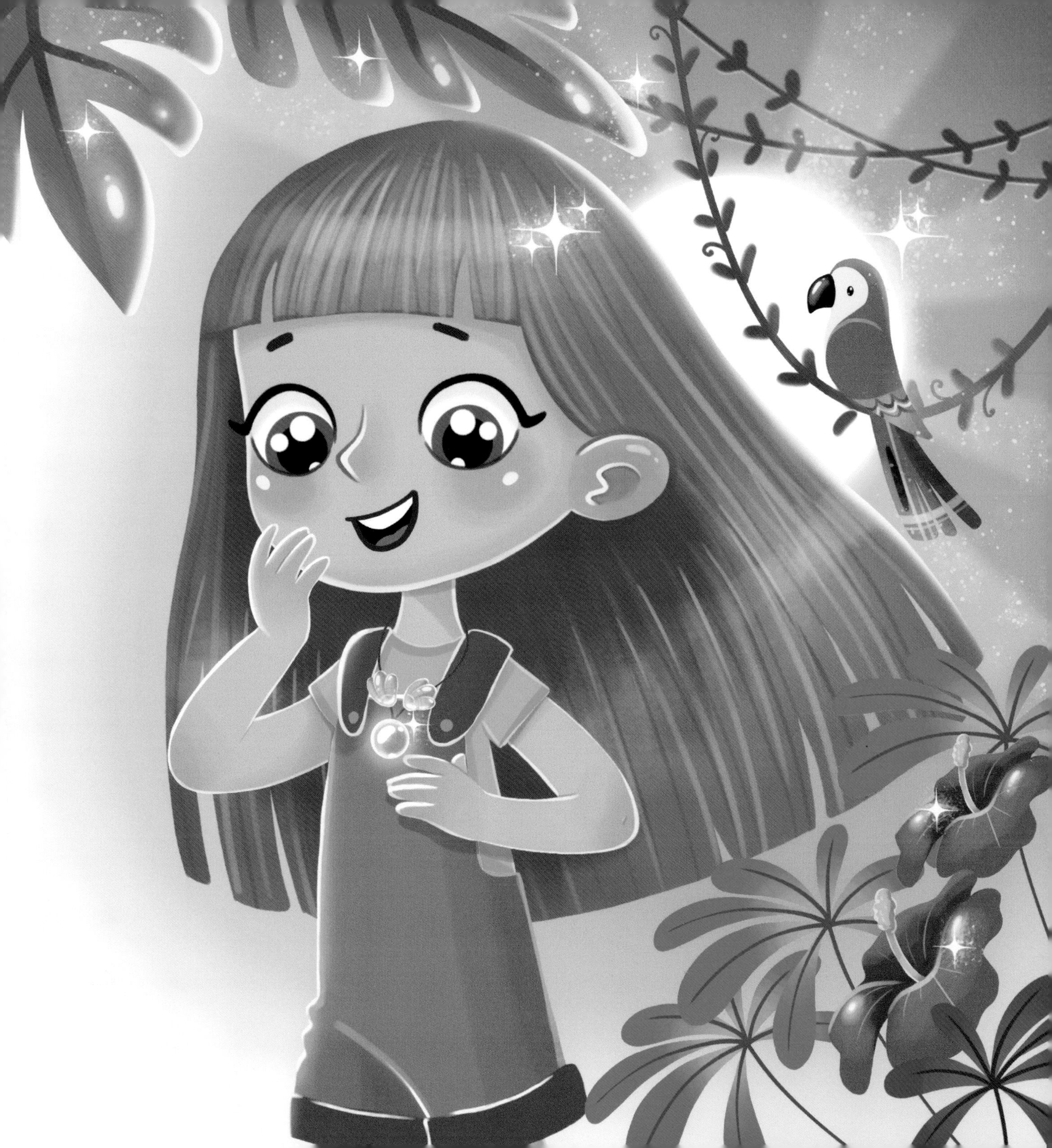

"Time to go, kids!" Dad calls from the beach's edge.

"I'll never forget this, Luna!" Aspen calls out to her new friend.

Luna makes a big splash as she swims away.

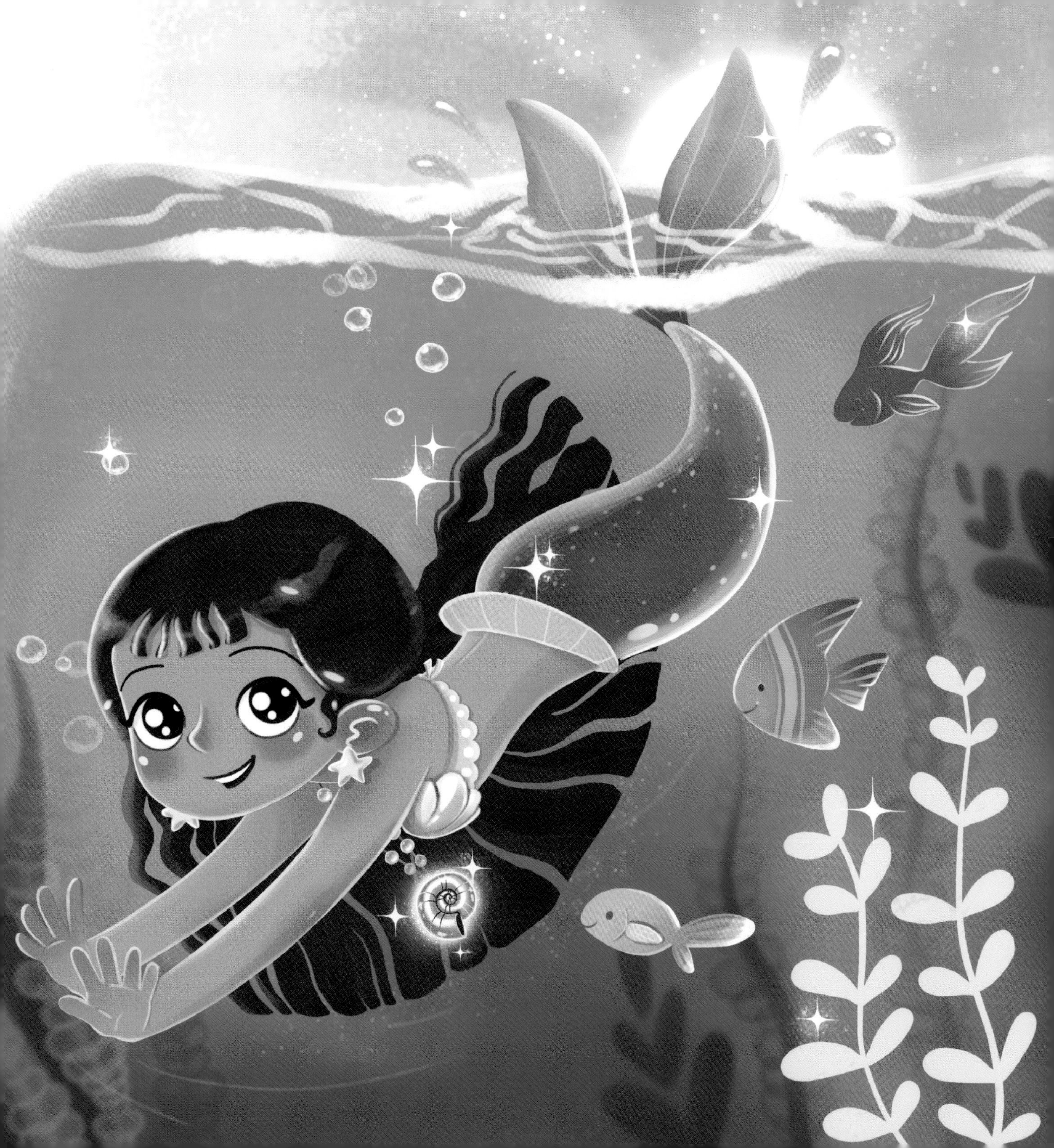

"Where is your necklace?" asks Easton.

"I found the owner and returned it. She needs it more than I do. But she gave me this one," explains Aspen. "Isn't it beautiful?"

"That's really cool you found her and gave it back," replies Easton.

"Aspen, we are so proud of you for doing the right thing and returning the necklace," agrees Dad.

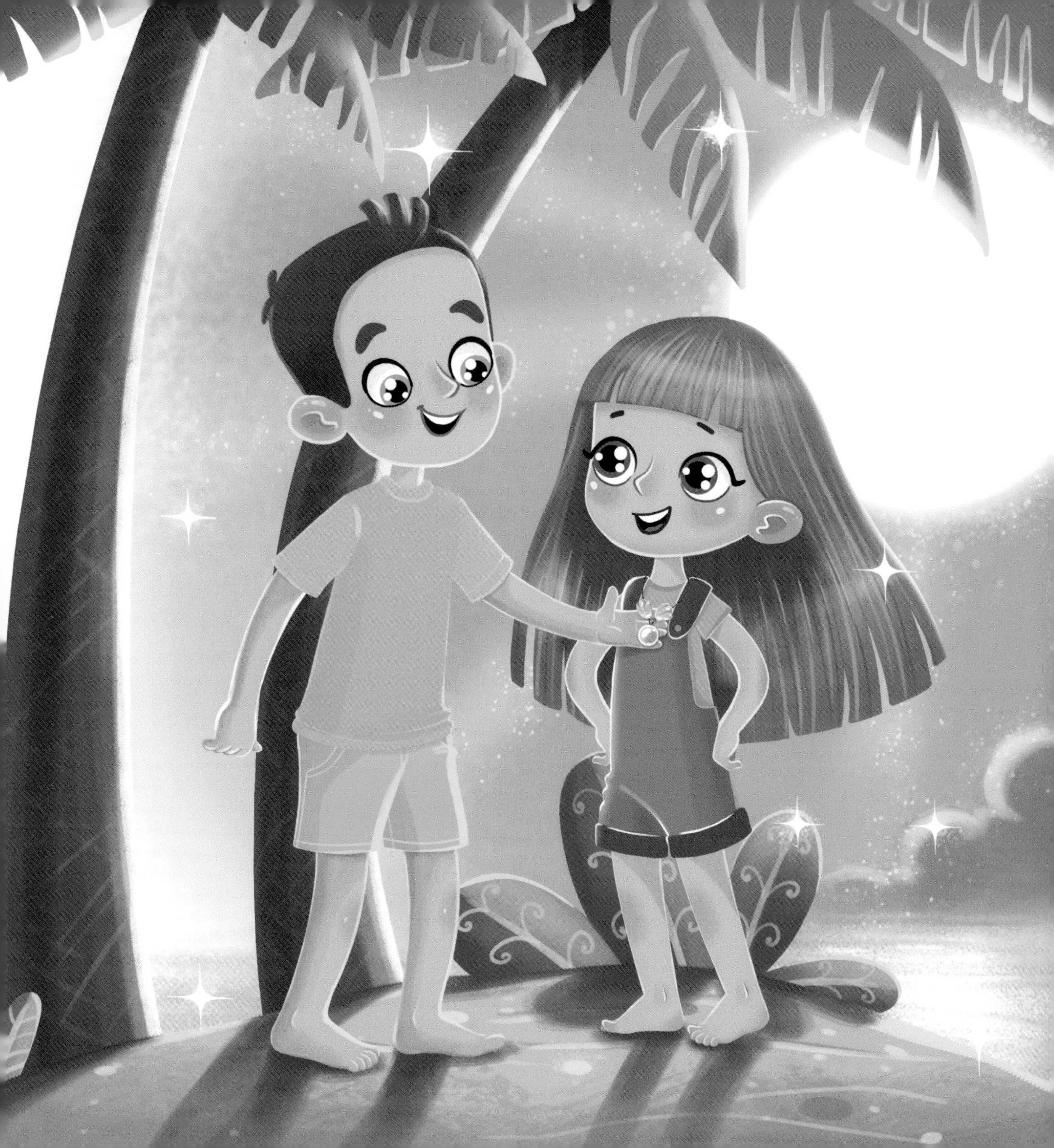

"What a great week! I think we need to make this an annual family vacation," declares Dad.

"Oh, yes! Then I can see Luna again!" exclaims Aspen.

"Luna?" Mom asks.

"My new friend, Mom. When can we come back?" Aspen smiles, imagining everything she and Luna will do when they see each other again.

"Soon," Mom assures. "Very soon."

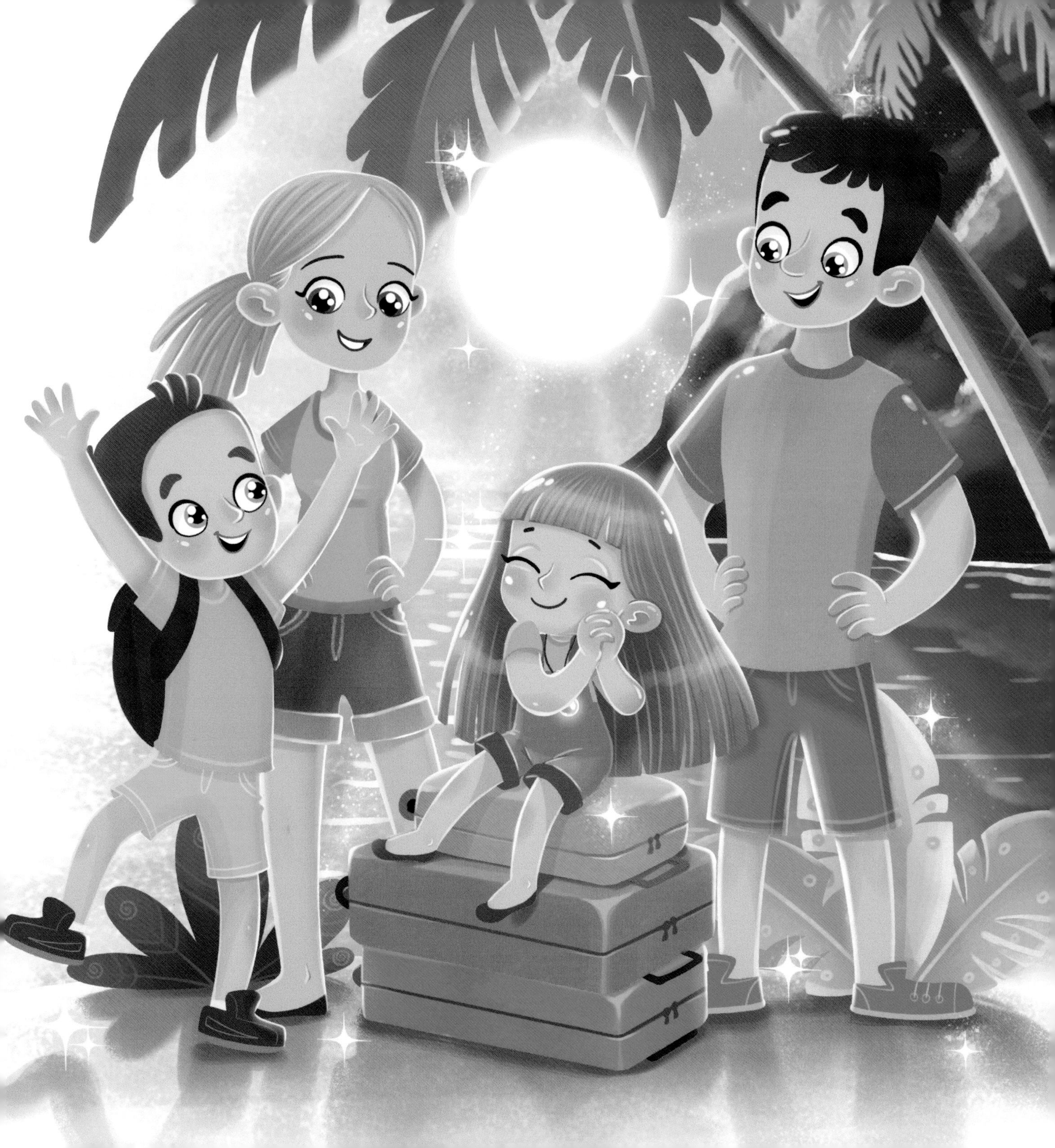

Make your very own Shell necklace.

Materials needed:

-  Medium-sized shell (pre-drilled if possible)
- Paints and paintbrush
- Jewelry cord or necklace chain
- Glitter
- Additional shells or pearls (optional)

1 Dab paint over your shell.

2 While still wet, sprinkle the shell with glitter. Let dry.

3 String the jewelry cord or necklace chain through the shell hole.

4 Add smaller shells or pearls along both sides of the shell for a larger necklace (optional).

5 Tie or clasp your new necklace around your neck and be the magical mermaid you know you are!

ABOUT THE AUTHOR

Melissa grew up in a creative and imaginative home in Karlsruhe, North Dakota. She spent her days playing outdoors on the farm, where her imagination led her to write endless stories. Well after bedtime, she hid beneath her covers, reading books by flashlight. Melissa resides in Lincoln, ND, with her husband and their two children.

Melissa draws inspiration from her two children as well as her spirited and mischievous childhood days on the farm. She loves writing about being the best you that you can be and finding the magic in the everyday. When not writing, you will find her chasing after her children, cheering in the hockey rink, and enjoying the outdoors.

Find her online at www.melissaahonen.com

ABOUT THE ILLUSTRATOR

Daria began her illustrating adventure at the age of 14 when she was hired for her first job at a newspaper created by teenagers. She later studied at her local University and began professionally publishing soon after. Daria has illustrated multiple children's books and has a special talent for creating adorable, colorful and bright characters.

Daria resides in the Ukraine with her son, Daniel. He is the greatest love of her life! Becoming a mommy has made all her dreams come true. Daria's favorite activity is going to the zoo with her son and enjoying the many different types of animals together.